Library Learning Information

Idea Store® Bow
1 Gladstone Place
Roman Road
London E3 5ES

020 7364 4332

Created and managed by
Tower Hamlets Council

AXIS education

Acknowledgements

Cover design: Oliver Heath, Rafters Design

Brinsford books are a direct result of the findings of a two-year authoring/research project with young offenders at HMYOI Brinsford, near Wolverhampton. Grateful thanks go to all the young people who participated so enthusiastically in the project and to Judy Jackson and Brian Eccleshall of Dudley College of Technology.

First published in Great Britain by Axis Education Ltd

ISBN 1-903685-99-0

Axis Education PO Box 459
Shrewsbury SY4 4WZ

Email: enquiries@axiseducation.co.uk

www.axiseducation.co.uk

Chapter One

"I don't know, Max. I've got no money for Gemma's birthday. She's set her heart on a pair of roller blades. I'm having enough trouble paying for food this week."

Mrs Jones's mouth was set in a thin line. She hardly ever laughed these days.

"Something will turn up, Mum."

"So you keep saying. Now don't you go doing anything stupid."

"I don't know what you mean, Mum."

Max walked off with a knowing grin.

He raced upstairs and nearly tripped on the threadbare carpet in his room. "Man, this place is a mess! I can't have Mum worrying. Where are my screwdrivers? I'll need a glass hammer too."

Tower Hamlets	
Suppliers Code AVA	
Price	£4.95
Invoice Date	01/11/2006
LOC	BOW
Class	428.6
Barcode	C001277948

Max slipped the tools into the back pocket of his jeans and ran out of the house.

"See ya later, Mum!" he shouted as the front door slammed behind him.

He strode into town, checking out the cars as he went. Nothing worth nicking in his neighbourhood. But he knew just where to go. The shopping car park near the football stadium was usually a good place to start. Well, his mum needed the money, didn't she? And it was Gemma's 13th birthday. That was something special and she deserved a good present. At least this time he would be nicking in a good cause. Mind you, he could do with a bag. No, not today. He had business to attend to first.

Max's speciality was face off stereos. He didn't bother with any other kind. He walked down the road, bending to look through the car windows. He didn't care who saw him. Besides, he wouldn't be long. The third car he came to was a Ford Orion with a blanking plate where the stereo should be. His eagle eyes spotted the Kenwood logo in the right hand corner of the black plastic. Yes, a Kenwood Mask. He'd get at least £80 for that.

He didn't hesitate. He smashed the window with the glass hammer and reached in through the window to open the door.

The shattered safety glass crunched underneath his jeans as Max leapt into the seat. He whipped the screwdrivers out of his pockets. He jammed the tools either side of the plate and tried to wrench out the stereo. It was tough, but he knew it would give. He twisted the screwdrivers harder and prised the stereo out. Then he yanked the wires out of the back of the dashboard. He stashed the stereo into his Aldi bag and sprang out of the car.

Max stuffed the bag up his Fila jacket and walked up the street. He looked as if he didn't have a care in the world but his heart was beating wildly. What a buzz! It had only taken 90 seconds – it must be a record!

Chapter Two

Ten minutes later Max got home with a grin on his face.

"Where've you been? You had at least half a dozen calls from different girls." In spite of the worry in her eyes his Mum couldn't help a quick smile. "The first one said she was called Emma and I didn't bother getting the rest down. You're going to get yourself in trouble with all these girls, Max."

"Just tell them to stop calling, Mum. They're not important. Anyway, I've got Gemma's birthday sorted, so you can stop worrying about that."

Max's mother rolled her eyes. "Just spare me the details."

She carried on with the ironing. The pile of crumpled clothes never seemed to get any smaller.

"Do you want to buy a stereo?" Max asked Sunny.

"Let's have a look."

Max handed the Kenwood over. Sunny paid good prices and was always on the look out for a deal.

"I want £80 for it."

"That seems fair." Sunny took a roll of notes as big as a grapefruit out of his pocket. He was never short of money. Max noticed that Sunny's other pocket was bulging too. Sunny counted out four crisp twenty pound notes.

Max couldn't keep his eyes off the other pocket. He handed back one of the notes. "Go on. I'll have one bag and a tenner back instead."

"I didn't think you could resist." Sunny passed Max a bag with a small amount of brown powder wrapped in a Rizzla.

"See you around, then." Max couldn't wait to get back to his room. He'd been dreaming of this all day.

Finally home and upstairs, he searched for his tin foil. It was under the bed, hidden from his Mum. He knew the feeling he was about to get and he was buzzing.

Max opened the wrap and put some brown on the foil. As he burned it with his lighter the powder turned to liquid and he started to suck the smack. It was good and he started to feel the high.

He lay back on his bed in a daze. Nothing mattered when he felt like this. He could forget living in this miserable little house and having no money. He was on top of the world, thanks to a little bag of brown. Instant happiness, and it only cost a tenner.

A tenner! Shit! Now he needed to make up the rest of the money for Gemma's birthday. After he'd promised the money from the stereo was all for her too! Max felt bad. Well, he'd just have to go out and rob a bit more.

His head was dizzy by now and he wasn't really thinking straight. Heroin always made him hyper. And reckless.

Max ran into town. He only needed a tenner and she looked like a rich bitch.

He ran up behind the girl in the long leather coat. He grabbed her wrist and held a cold knife against her stomach.

"Hand over your purse!" He almost yelled it. The mixture of smack and adrenalin made him edgy. "Now!"

The girl looked terrified. He barely noticed. She rummaged in her bag.

"Come on." His voice was squeaky now. "Just give me the fucking money."

He snatched the purse out of her hand and tore off down the street.

"You're scum!" he heard the girl shout. But no one chased him. He could feel the eyes of onlookers boring into him, but no one dared to get involved. As usual.

By the time he got home his heartbeat had gone back to normal. There was £40 in the purse. More than enough for Gemma's present. She'd have a great day now.

The image of the girl in the leather coat appeared in Max's mind. Had she been that scared? He pushed the thought to the back of his mind.

He put aside the eighty pounds for Gemma's present and smiled. He couldn't wait to see her face when she opened that present. It would be worth it.

Chapter Three

Gemma's birthday came and went and Max had started to see this girl. He didn't really like her. She just gave him constant grief. He didn't know why he bothered really, apart from the obvious.

A gang of them were in his mum's living room and the girl started on at him again. He was well fed up.

"You just nag, nag, nag," he said.

She hurled another insult at him. In front of all his friends, it was just too much.

"Just fuck off. Go on, get out," he said.

She grabbed her coat and spat at him. "You're a useless tosser anyway."

They all laughed. "That's the older woman for you, Max," said his mate Chris. "They don't want you to act like a kid, you know."

Max laughed. Maybe they were right. She was quite a bit older than him. He looked around. Lisa was looking nice.

"So, Lisa." He sat down next to her. "You and me linking up or what?"

"No," she said, but she smiled too. He'd known Lisa for ages. He used to see her around a lot. When Max and his brothers used to drink on the wall outside, she'd been one of the girls who'd always stop and chat.

He'd never really noticed she was so pretty. She had grown up a bit and he always felt she had liked him. He looked at her and grinned. She smiled back shyly. Yes, she fancied him. He was sure.

He teased her and joked with her. She'd play hard to get, of course. But by the time she left, they'd be going out.

There was just one problem.

"Come on, Lisa. I know you like me."

"Yeah, but there's more to it than that." Lisa frowned down at the varnish on her fingernails.

"What do you mean?"

She looked up from her nails and stared him straight in the eye. "You're a dickhead for doing what you do. And I don't want nothing to do with all that."

"It's nothing, and I've never been caught."

"Maybe not yet."

"What if I say I'll cut out the drugs?"

"And the crime?"

She was worth it. "Okay. That too," he told her.

They started going out that afternoon.

Chapter Four

But Max didn't keep his promises.

It was too hard. He couldn't give up the smack. He knew Lisa was special. He'd never felt like this about a girl before. But the drugs had a hold on him too.

Four months after he started to go out with Lisa he was caught doing a street robbery. Lisa took it badly, but he was expecting a probation order.

The court hearing came up quickly and Lisa stood by him all the way.

Max stood in the dock in the Magistrates Court with his eyes firmly fixed on the floor.

"I'm sentencing you to 14 months' imprisonment."

Max couldn't believe his ears. The magistrate just sat and looked at him as if he were the scum of the earth. The sentence would feel like a lifetime with no Lisa and no smack.

★★★★★★★★★★★★★★★★★★★★★★★★★★★★★★★★★★★★

Doing time wasn't as hard as he thought. Lisa's letters kept him going. She wrote every single day. She visited him each week. She kept him sane.

"One good thing about jail, Lisa." He bent over and held her hand.

"Yeah?"

"I'm clean."

"I've heard it before, Max."

"Really, no smack. Not since I've been inside. I reckon I've beaten it."

"I hope so, Max. I don't know what I'd do if you came in this place again." Lisa shuddered as she looked around her at the other visitors and inmates. "It's no place for me, Max."

"I know. You deserve better."

Chapter Five

The arguing started when Max got out of prison. Just when he thought things were going to be okay.

Lisa started getting naggy. In fact she sometimes went completely mental. She got jealous and angry, and quickly too. Sometimes she even frightened Max. She was always on at him for things.

When they went to town, she'd look in the shop windows and tug his arm.

"That's nice, Max."

"Yeah, yeah." He tried to brush off her hand.

"I really like it," she whined.

"Maybe I'll get it for you for Christmas."

"But I want it now. Come on, Max. Won't you buy it for me?" She tried to wheedle it out of him every time. It just made him mad. He'd heard enough. He stormed off, fuming.

Later that night Max went out robbing. It was the only way to make her happy, buying her things. He burgled three sheds and got £100 from Sunny for the tools. That'd be enough for Lisa's watch.

He bought it for her the next day. He got nicked for the burglaries that night.

Lisa had the brass neck to go mental at him. "Where've you been?"

"Down the police station. I've been done again."

Lisa's face went red and her eyes looked as if they were on fire. She slapped Max across the face. He turned away.

"Don't you walk away when I'm talking to you!"

"You're not talking, Lisa. You're just losing it."

She grabbed an ashtray off the table and hurled it at his head. It just missed his ear and hit the wall behind him.

"You're a stupid bitch. I did it for you!"

Lisa was heading for him again. Max decided to leg it.

Two days later she had some news.

"Max, I'm pregnant."

"Are you sure?"

"'Course I am."

"Look, Lisa, I'm not sure we're ready for all this. We're having enough trouble as it is. Don't you think it'll spoil our relationship?"

"No. It'll be fine."

"I'm not sure we'll be able to cope."

Chapter Six

Max got six months for the shed burglaries. Lisa stood by him as she'd said she would. The letters and visits came and Max started to get really excited about the baby. He would have to get a job when he got out.

Max was lucky. He walked into a job the day he got out. He found work on a building site, starting on £25 a day. It wasn't much, but he was claiming benefit on top, so it all added up. He needed all the money he could get for Lisa and the baby.

Work wasn't all it was cracked up to be, though. He had to carry wheelbarrows full of bricks up and down stairs all day. Max came home exhausted each evening. The baby was due in just over three months and there was still a lot to get. He wanted his baby to have the very best.

A few weeks into the job things were working out fine. He was saving money and sort of enjoying work. He had a laugh with the other lads. Too much of a laugh, in fact.

One Friday they were messing about throwing bricks. The other lads must have seen the boss coming, but Max didn't. Just as the boss turned the corner a brick left Max's hand and whistled past the boss's ear.

"You, Max!" he yelled, his face crimson. "You can leave right now."

"But I was only messing ..."

"Not in my time. Go on, get out."

Max left. He'd have to break it to Lisa. She'd be furious.

Chapter Seven

A week later they were at Chris's house.

"My stomach's killing me," complained Lisa.

"You're not eating properly. It's hunger pains. I'll cook you something."
Max went into the kitchen and made Lisa a big fry-up.

"Here, eat up." He handed her a plate.

Lisa tucked in, but she didn't look right.

"It still hurts, Max, and I need the loo."

She came back five minutes later. "I feel constipated and there was
blood, too. I'm scared, Max."

Max felt ill. Was she having the baby? It was way too early. He
grabbed Chris's mobile to call an ambulance. She couldn't lose the
baby, not now.

The five-minute wait for the ambulance felt like an hour.

At the maternity unit a doctor gave Lisa an internal examination. He looked serious.

"There's no time to move you. You're going to have to push right now."

The baby boy was delivered just five minutes later. Max cried with happiness when he saw him. He felt on top of the world, even though the baby was so small.

The tiny boy was taken straight to the neonatal unit. He only weighed two pounds and thirteen ounces and was almost three months premature. Little Harry would need to stay in hospital for a while yet.

Max was dedicated to his boy. He visited the hospital each day without fail. Which was more than he could say for Lisa. She seemed to have lost interest in the baby. She also started nagging again. This time she wanted an engagement ring.

"Go on, Max. We've got a baby now. I really want a ring," Lisa griped.

"You know we can't afford it right now."

"Come on, Max. Don't I deserve one?"

"Look, I've told you, Lisa, now is not the time. We're going to need all the money we can get when Harry gets out of hospital."

"But I want a ring." Lisa looked at him sulkily.

"Fuck you, Lisa, you're doing my head in."

Max stormed off. Same old story, he thought to himself. She's just taking the piss. But I want to keep her happy.

Later that afternoon Max did a job and bought her a damn ring. He'd tell her it wasn't an engagement ring, though. It would keep her happy – for a while at least.

The next day Max and Chris went to collect some bags of baby clothes from Lisa's old flat. The guy who lived there now had looked after them for her.

When they got back to Max's they found one of the bags was full of PlayStation games. Max smiled. No need to hand these back. He could get a fair bit from Sunny for these.

Later that night Chris told Max that the bloke who had given them back the bags had reported them to the police for theft.

It wasn't fair! He'd been given them, hadn't he? It wasn't his fault that the guy had handed over the wrong bag!

Max would have to lie low for a bit. He knew just the place. The house next to his mum's was empty and they could get to it from the loft. He could stay there for a bit. Lisa went to her mum's.

After a few days Max got lazy. Next door wasn't as comfy as his mum's. He decided to stay at home instead. Mum and Gemma were away for a week.

Before they went to sleep Max and his two brothers Kevin and Rob barricaded the front door. His mum had just had a new cooker delivered so they jammed that against the front door and put a settee and chair behind it.

Chapter Eight

Boom!

It was early next morning. The noise sounded like a battering ram.
It took them a couple of moments to realise what was going on.

"Shit! It's the cops!"

Max ran out of the room and met the others on the landing. Pieces of
the front door splintered past their makeshift barricade.
The noise was deafening.

"The loft!"

They all headed upstairs to escape into the loft. The police weren't far behind. Max turned his head. They had truncheons and it looked as if there were at least six of them. He scrambled up the hatch and made his way across the beams.

"Fuck! The way out's blocked up!" They were trapped.

"Come down. We know you're up there."

They stayed quiet and still. Max edged his way to the darkest corner he could find.

The police came up through the hatch.

"Aargh!" He could hear Rob yelling as the police were kicking him. They were all shouting and it was very confusing. They caught Kevin and threw him down the hatch. The yelling was deafening. Max thought he heard the pigs say they were going to shoot him. He wouldn't put it past them.

Best I come quietly then, he thought.

They were all taken to the station and held for a day.

"I admit keeping the stuff, but I don't admit burglary," Max told the cops. It made no difference. He was charged with burglary anyway.

The next day Max was bailed to a hostel by the magistrate. The hostel was miles away. How would he get to see Harry from there?

He ignored the order and stayed home.

Chapter Nine

Max knew he'd be caught in the end, but in the meantime he'd make the most of seeing Harry. The little boy was making good progress and getting bigger by the day. It wouldn't be long before he was out of hospital.

An old friend came to see him one evening.

Gary had always stood by Max in the past, so he could hardly refuse to return the favour. They took a short cut to the pub through the market. It was dark and the stalls looked spooky.

Max heard steps behind him. "There's one of them!" shouted a voice just a few steps away.

Max turned to look. A huge man wearing thick glasses loomed above Max's face. Before he had a chance to think he felt a clenched fist smack against the side of his head.

He reeled backwards and sized the bloke up. Max knew he had his stick on him. He needed to buy a little time.

"I dare you to punch me again."

"You what?"

"Go on. I dare you."

The bloke looked astonished. The stick Max smashed into the centre of his face wiped away his smile. His glasses shattered into tiny pieces and sprinkled on the ground. The man fell to the ground with a heavy thud. He was knocked clean out.

Max looked up. Gary was busy fighting another bloke. He glanced backwards. The market was opposite the police station. Had he been spotted?

He ran round the back of the shops. His heart sank. There'd always been one cop that had it in for him. And there he was. Max dived behind the bins. Hopefully he had got away with it.

No such luck.

A uniformed arm reached in front of him and a large hand grabbed his shoulder.

"Get out, Jones."

Chapter Ten

This time they made sure Max was kept off the streets. He was remanded into custody at a Young Offenders Institution.

How would this go down with Lisa?

She came to visit him during his first week. But she wasn't alone. His mate Chris had tagged along too. The visits room was packed.

Lisa cried when she saw him. But when he hugged and kissed her Max could tell that something was wrong.

"I love you," he told her.

Lisa avoided his gaze. Max had butterflies in his stomach. There was more to this than just him being in jail. He knew it. His gut feelings were never wrong.

They talked about Harry and about nothing in particular until Chris went off to chat to another mate. Max was sure she'd tell him what it was when they were alone. But when he asked her she said nothing.

As he walked back to his cell Max felt happy that Lisa had visited. But deep down he knew that something was very wrong.

Two days later he got a letter.

"I love you more than all my heart, Max. I'm missing you loads. I want things to change. I want us to stop arguing."

The letter went on saying the same things in different ways.

He got the message. That night he rang Lisa.

"I've written you a letter," she told him.

"I know. I've got it."

"No. Another one."

He had a cold feeling in his stomach. "What's it about?"

"Just read it."

He had to know. "Is it about finishing with me?" he asked shakily.

There was a long pause. "Yes. Max, things just aren't working out."

Max felt sick. Tears streamed down his face. The lads waiting to use the phone looked away. All he could think about was the baby. Harry needed his Dad. If Lisa broke contact with him, he'd hardly ever see him. He tried to pull himself together. He couldn't really think straight.

"Lisa, I can't talk any more. We'll have to leave it at that. But I want you to know that I'll never stop loving you and Harry."

He hung up. Any other time, lads would have taunted him for crying over a girl. They must have been able to tell it was serious. As he walked past the queue several boys patted him on the shoulder and made sympathetic comments.

"Gutted, mate."

It was no comfort. He felt like he wanted to die. Darren, one of his friends, looked after him and tried to get him to talk.

"I'm really worried about you, Max. You shouldn't be on your own, mate."

"I don't care. No one loves me any more. I can't take it. I just don't see the point in carrying on."

Darren went off and talked to the officers on the wing. That night they arranged for Darren to share Max's cell.

"You that worried about me?" Max asked through his tears.

"I've never seen you so bad before, Max. I just don't want you doing anything stupid."

Max was glad of the company, but Lisa was preying on his mind all the time. Daytimes weren't too bad because he was busy. In classes during the day he'd try to blank it out by laughing and joking and trying to do anything except be serious. Nights were different. He'd cry himself to sleep worrying about not being a family and having to leave Harry.

Why was she doing this now? Max was sure there must be someone else.

Chapter Eleven

Max had to find out what was really going on with Lisa. He decided to bluff her. He called her again. After a bit of small talk, he cut to the chase.

"Lisa, look there's something I've been meaning to tell you. It's been happening for over a year now."

"What are you talking about?"

"I've been with someone else," Max lied.

"Who is it, then?" Her voice started to rise.

"I'm not saying."

"Well, guess what, Max. I've been seeing someone too." Lisa sounded aggressive.

"Well, you tell me who it is and then I'll tell you who mine is."

"It's Chris."

"I fucking knew it!" Max felt as if he was going to explode. "You fucking slag! With Chris! He's my best mate! You've stooped low this time, you bitch. I'm going to fucking kill you when I get out of here!" He ranted and raged at her, oblivious to the fuss going on around him.

Three officers pushed the lads around the phone away. As Max turned to look, the hand piece was snatched away from him and smacked against his face. Someone else cut him off.

"Calm down, Jones."

Max was in no mood for chit chat. "My girl's done the dirty on me with my best friend and you want me to calm down?"

"We know what's going on. It's all on tape."

"What the hell for?"

"Threatening to kill someone."

Max was still seething when they shoved him back into his cell. He'd known something was wrong. As he calmed down he tried to analyse it. At the back of his mind, he'd always known Lisa and Chris couldn't be trusted together. He'd just been denying it to himself.

What could he do? He still loved her, in spite of everything.

He made up his mind. "Whatever happens, I'm not losing Lisa, and I'm not losing my son."

Chapter Twelve

Max couldn't stop thinking about Lisa. She was like a drug. He was addicted to her, and now he was having withdrawal symptoms. He managed to last three days before he called her again.

She sounded cool and distant. "What do you want, Max?"

"I want you to get back with me."

"You know it won't work out."

"We can start again, Lisa. We can forget all this and make a fresh start."

"We just argue all the time."

"Only when you go on at me for things. And that's how come I'm in here. I want to make you happy, Lisa. Me not being able to give you things makes you disappointed. I don't want that. So you ask and I go and get – whatever it takes. That's what won't work."

"Max, we just don't make each other happy."

"Maybe. The only times we don't argue are when I buy you things or when we're in bed."

"Exactly. It won't work. It can't work. We just argue too much."

"Lisa, I ..."

She hung up. Max was beside himself and choked back the tears. How low had he sunk? Begging her to come back to him. He wasn't proud. At least not any more. Over the last few minutes he'd lost every ounce of pride he ever had.

As he walked away from the phone the lad next in line to make a call was laughing at him.

Max's face twisted into grimace. "Don't fucking laugh at me, you prick!"

"Shut up, loser," the lad shouted back.

"I'll knock you out. Do you think I fucking care? My girl's just ended it with me. Do you think I care about doing extra days for a prick like you?"

Max was shaking with anger and misery. Darren tugged at his arm. He shook it loose.

He stormed off down the corridor and booted a bin. Papers went flying everywhere. He didn't notice. He could hardly see for the tears. He'd lost Lisa. He'd probably lost Harry too. And for what?

Gutted.

Glossary

brown   heroin

rizzla   cigarette paper

smack   heroin